A PLACE BY THE FIRE

Also by William MacKellar

A DOG LIKE NO OTHER
GHOST IN THE CASTLE
A GOAL FOR GREG
WEE JOSEPH
TWO FOR THE FAIR

A PLACE

BY THE

FIRE

By WILLIAM MacKELLAR

illustrated by Ursula Koering

DAVID McKAY COMPANY, Inc.   NEW YORK

A PLACE BY THE FIRE

COPYRIGHT © 1966 BY WILLIAM MACKELLAR

LIBRARY OF CONGRESS CATALOG CARD NUMBER: 66-13112

MANUFACTURED IN THE UNITED STATES OF AMERICA

VAN REES PRESS • NEW YORK

FOR

Davie Duncan

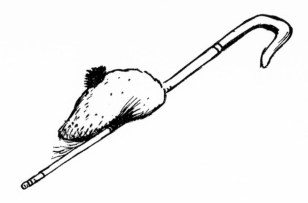

CONTENTS

A PLACE BY THE FIRE

1. A Dog Grows Old

For the fourth time that afternoon Donald caught his eyes drawn curiously to the grim face of his stepfather. Plainly there was something on his mind. Something scarcely pleasant. Or so it would seem from the frown that pinched the loose skin between the hard blue eyes. His lips were set in a firm, straight line too, a clear sign that Finlay MacNab was annoyed.

The boy hesitated. He would have liked to have asked what was wrong. Only his stepfather was not the sort of man who invited idle questions. Nor had

he ever been. Although Donald could scarcely remember his own father any more, Ian Fraser who
had gone down with his fishing boat, he still clung
to a memory of a dark face and a quick smile. Few
smiles, quick or otherwise ever touched the grim
face of this man who had married his mother a year
ago. Nor was it simply because Finlay MacNab was
much older than his mother and set in his ways. It
was more than that. From that first day Donald had
resented his presence in the little cottage he had
shared with his mother. He still resented it.

Yet granted that his stepfather was a dour man
with no smiles to him at all, it was still plain to see
that something was on the old shepherd's mind.
Donald tried another tack.

"A grand day, is it no?" he remarked. His stepfather could hardly argue with *that*. For late October in Scotland it was more than just grand. It was
unnatural. A brilliant sun blazed down from a cloudless sky. High flying birds, trailing bright ribbons
of song behind them, soared southwards. The
heather-shaggy glen seemed to throb gently in the
glare of the late sun.

Finlay MacNab did not answer. He was not looking at the birds. Or the glen. His eyes, thin slits
with hard blue behind them, were fastened on the

dog. On Tam. The scruffy little black and white Border collie plodded slowly, almost painfully behind the sheep. Almost as though he was tired. But then that should scarcely have been surprising. After all, Tam was no longer a young dog. In fact, he was a very old dog. The oldest sheep dog in all the countryside around the village of Cairnsmore.

Suddenly Donald noticed the strange ram with the great curved horns edging towards the flock of ewes. It was not one of Colonel Chisholm's tups. The dark face had been dyed a bright yellow to make it more conspicuous and it had a large green L on its back rather than the red C which identified the sheep of Colonel Chisholm for whom Finlay MacNab herded. Even if for some reason it had belonged to the colonel it had no business here. The colonel was proud of his pure Cheviot ewes. He wanted no mixture of blood that might in any way debase the soft, fine fleece of his Cheviots.

Finlay MacNab spotted the intruder at the same moment. An exclamation of wrath burst from his lips. He emitted a loud, clear "wheep" from between his teeth and lips, a signal for Tam, some distance to his right, to rush back and cut off the tup from the others. Perhaps it was the wind blowing against him from the hills that prevented Tam from hear-

ing the whistle. Perhaps it was simply that his sense
of hearing, once so keen, had become blunted by
time. Perhaps that was it. At any rate, the old dog
continued to plod along, oblivious to the danger to
his charges.

Finlay MacNab's face darkened. Angrily he thrust
his arm outwards in a wide sweeping motion. If
Tam could not hear him he could at least see him.
But Tam did not see him. Tam, whose eyes had once
been the sharpest of any dog around Cairnsmore,
did not catch the signal. Head low, he moved slowly
behind a few stragglers, his mind apparently on

other matters. Perhaps the bowl of gruel awaiting him at the end of the day. Perhaps the good feeling of easing his old bones into the wicker basket in his place by the fire.

Finlay MacNab waited no longer. Brandishing his shepherd's crook over his head like a Highlander's broadsword, he rushed after the intruder, now only a few yards from the sheep. It was only then that Tam seemed to sense the danger. Finally catching his master's furious gestures he wheeled to his right and was off in a wide sweep to cut off the ugly faced ram.

"Grip him, Tam!" yelled Donald's stepfather, giving the command which is only used in moments of

peril. Rushing low through the nettles and rough grass, Tam made for the intruder. The ram spotted his approach, lowered his great horns, then thinking better of it turned and fled. Tam pursued him for about a hundred yards, then, seemingly tiring of the chase, he halted and trotted back to his master. The dog's frosted muzzle wrinkled as he breathed heavily, his mouth open.

The boy said quickly when his stepfather didn't speak, "There was no harm done at all."

The shepherd's lips moved. "Aye. But no thanks to the dog." He spoke harshly. He paused, then said on a quieter note, "Still it will not be the dog's fault! He is old just."

"Aye, but just the same there will not be his like with the sheep. Tam still knows them better than any dog in Cairnsmore."

The shepherd didn't bother to answer the boy. Perhaps he hadn't even heard him. Suddenly he seemed to come to a decision. "It was fine that it happened this way with no harm at all to the sheep. Next week I will go and buy a dog. A young one. I'm thinking I should have got rid of Tam a while ago."

Donald stared. As long as he had known Finlay MacNab, Tam and he had gone out with the sheep.

"Come, Tam, we'll away and look the hill," was the way his stepfather always put it. And off they went together, fair weather or foul, to look the hill. Tam had known no master other than Donald's step-father. The dog had moved into their cottage when Finlay MacNab married Donald's mother. Donald had often reflected that it was the only good thing the grim-faced shepherd had brought with him. And now this! What kind of man was this who could announce in so matter-of-fact a way that he was going to get rid of his old dog and bring in another?

The boy picked his way carefully through the words that crowded his tongue. No sense in crossing his stepfather. He said, "It would break Tam's heart, I'm thinking, if you got another dog to take his place."

"Aye," said Finlay MacNab calmly. "It would."

"Always he's gone out with you to look the hill."

"Always."

"He has his pride, has Tam."

"Aye, he has that. As has any good dog." Finlay MacNab paused. "But we will not be needing him anymore after the new dog gets to know the sheep. Besides it would be a cruel thing indeed to have him sit by and watch another take his place. As you said, boy, he has his pride, has Tam."

Donald suddenly thought of something. A triumphant grin split his face. "Och, and you're forgetting something! Tam is so old there's no one would have him in Cairnsmore! If he'll no longer be able to take care of your sheep, he'll not be able to take care of anyone else's. So you'll not be able to give him away at all!"

Finlay MacNab said quietly, too quietly, "Aye, that is so, boy."

"Then don't you see? If you can't give Tam away—" He caught the look on his stepfather's face and the torrent of words backed up in his mouth as though a dam had suddenly been raised against them.

The thin lips moved. "Perhaps the fault will be mine that you do not know me better, boy. I am not a man who hides behind words like a fleeing thief behind heather. No one will take Tam. And it would be cruel just to keep Tam with another dog taking his place. So what happens to Tam will be best for Tam. Aye, and best for everyone. I will hear no more talk about it."

"But—"

The heavy brows gathered together. "You heard me, boy!" his stepfather snapped. "I will hear no more talk about it. Now away with you and give your mother a hand with the cows. There will be peats too to be stacked before the day's done."

Donald opened his mouth and then closed it. After all, what good were words anyway? Of all the words in the world there were none that could reach the remote heart of Finlay MacNab.

His head bowed, he walked slowly away. Tam had looked up expectantly as the boy had turned to go. When the shepherd made no motion the dog had not stirred. Finlay MacNab was his master. Had always been his master. The shepherd told him when to go. When to return. And when to lie down and be still.

But it was thoughts of another stillness, the stillness of death that filled Donald's mind as he made his way along Glen Dunan to his home. For despite the brilliance of the sky and the lights that shimmered on the normally somber waters of Loch Lorne, there was death in the air. And all of a sudden Donald realized he hated this man who was his stepfather. This man so unlike the father he still remembered. This man so cold, so distant, so sure that everything he did was just and right.

The boy felt the shiver that snaked between his shoulder blades. If only there was something he could do! Yet deep in his heart was the awful knowl-

edge that there was nothing he could do, anyone could do. Finlay MacNab had spoken. He had decreed that there was no place for old Tam. Either by the fire or elsewhere. And Finlay MacNab's word was law.

On an impulse the boy stopped. He looked back in the direction from which he had just come. He could not see his stepfather. No doubt he was on the other side of the small brae that swept up from Glen Dunan. But he could see Tam. The small black and white Border collie stood out against the dull purple of the heather as he swung wide to drive in the ewes.

Yet only for a second was the dog visible. Then suddenly, as though he had never been, he had vanished behind the brae with Finlay MacNab.

And in all the vast wasteland that was Glen Dunan, as far as the eye could see, nothing stirred. Nothing moved.

2. Alec Has a Solution

Good day to you, Donald Fraser."

The boy wheeled around when he heard the voice. It was a voice he knew, yet where had it come from? His eyes, curious and alert, probed the clumps of waist-high bracken fronds nearby. There was no one there. Nor behind the few scrawny bramble bushes that lifted above the flatness of the land. Nowhere in all of solitary Glen Dunan was there a stir of life. Had he been daydreaming?

"Here, Donald, above your head."

Only then did he realize he was standing under

a tree, the only one in the whole sweep of the glen. He stared up and found two black-as-a-button eyes studying him gravely. The face was old, yet young. Seamed by time and weather, yet placid with the innocence of childhood. For although Wee Alec Logan was a man full grown, he would never be a full-grown man. Many might have considered him a dwarf, although actually he was not quite that small. No one knew for certain why Wee Alec had never grown. Now no one really cared. Wee Alec was Wee Alec, a familiar sight as he rolled on his small legs along High Street, on his way to the Cairnsmore *Weekly Press* where he worked as its reporter.

"Alec! It's yourself!" Donald exclaimed. "And what now will you be doing up there in a tree?"

The natty little man in the well cut herringbone tweed jacket with the mother-of-pearl buttons, considered the question for a moment before replying. "Maybe I just get tired of looking *up* at other people. Now and then I just feel like looking down at *them*." His thin high voice had carried no note of irony yet Donald had sensed the bitterness behind the words. There were some in the village who felt that Wee Alec preferred the company of children simply because they were the same size as he was. Perhaps, though, it was more than that. Perhaps it was simply that Wee Alec, having the quickest and cleverest mind in Cairnsmore, had decided a long time ago that hearing young people laugh was far more fun than listening to old people talk.

The little man swung himself down from the tree. He landed on all fours then quickly rose and beat the dust from his sharply creased slacks. Wee Alec was neat about his appearance, as he was neat about everything he did. He adjusted the Windsor knot on his silk tie and straightened the fresh white carnation in his buttonhole. All the time his quick eyes never left the boy.

"So, Donald Fraser, and what is wrong with you?" he demanded. "Here the good Lord gives Scotland in late October a day He seldom gives it in July and you go around with a face like a graveyard at midnight!"

"It's Tam," Donald answered bluntly.

"Tam?" Half of Wee Alec's face gathered in a frown. He closed one eye in concentration. "Finlay's dog?"

"Aye, the same. There is only one Tam."

"Of course." Wee Alec grinned. "And what about Tam?"

"My stepfather, he says Tam is too old for the sheep just."

The little man scratched his nose. He darted a keen glance at the boy. "That could be true, Donald. Tam is an old one. In his day, of course, there was none better in the Highlands." He paused. "Hmmmm. So Finlay MacNab will be getting himself a new dog, eh? It will seem strange to him after all the years he has gone out with Tam. But that is the way the world is."

"But Alec, he—he will not be keeping Tam after the new dog comes."

Alec said quickly, "Finlay will have to train the new dog. That takes time. He will still need Tam."

"Aye, but after the training, what then?" Donald swallowed hard and looked away.

"There will be no place for Tam," Alec Logan said. He studied the boy with his bird quick eyes. "You do not like Finlay MacNab?" he asked softly.

Donald said, "No." He was tempted to say more but held his tongue.

"That is not good, Donald. Still, you must not be hard on him because of this thing. Some shepherds keep their dogs in the byres with the cows and have little use for them when the day's work is done. Finlay MacNab is not like that. His dog shares his comforts as it shares his work. Besides Tam is a dog of spirit and pride. He would take it badly if another took his place. In fact it would be cruel to keep him. No, Donald, your stepfather does only what he thinks is right."

"Och," cried the boy, "but don't you see, Alec? There will not be anyone at all who will take Tam in! He's too old just."

Wee Alec sighed. "I do see, lad. You must remember that Cairnsmore is a poor village with poor people in it. They have little enough food for themselves without giving it away to a useless dog."

"And Tam?"

The little man shrugged a shoulder. "Your stepfather will know how to handle that. The dog will feel nothing." He paused and a small wry smile plucked at the corners of his mouth. "As I said, Donald Fraser, that is the way the world is. You should not be surprised at all that at times it can be a sad world. For wee dogs as well as wee men." The small, wry smile still played around his lips.

But Donald did not see the smile, hear the words. His thoughts were far away. In his mind's eye he could see Tam and the funny way he rolled when he walked. Tam curled up in his place by the fire. Tam standing still in the wet heather, the wind ruffling his black and white coat and making a brave banner of his plumed tail.

"It's not right!" he suddenly heard himself exclaim fiercely. "And I'm not caring if it's the way the world is! Tam's been a good sheep dog, aye, the best in Cairnsmore, and now because he's old there's no place for him at all!" He stopped for breath. "Alec, everyone knows there's none smarter than yourself in all Cairnsmore. Och, and you've got to think of something! You've just got to!"

Wee Alec opened his mouth then closed it again without saying anything. He scowled up at the cloudless sky. He scowled down at the ground. He scowled at Donald.

"You want to spare Tam's life?"

"Aye!" cried Donald eagerly.

"Even though it may mean grief for him, what with another dog taking his place?"

Donald said desperately, "I just don't want anything at all to happen to Tam. I just want him with us."

The little man sighed. "Very well, lad. Advice you want. Advice I give you. I warn you though, it is not advice I would take myself, knowing as I do the pride in old Tam." He looked off in the distance at Loch Lorne. "The proud suffer more."

But all Donald could cry was, "And what is the advice, Alec?"

"Pray," said Alec Logan.

"Eh?" Donald gasped.

"Pray," repeated the little man calmly. "But don't mumble it to yourself. It has to be in a loud, clear voice so that God can hear you." He stopped, seemed to think of something, then added, "By your bed in the kitchen."

Amazement gave way to resentment in Donald. The hopes so high, had come crashing to the ground. Just because Wee Alec was clever was no reason at all for the little man to make sport of him! Pray in a loud voice indeed! Aye as though the good Lord was hard of hearing!

Alec must have caught the look of disappointment on the boy's face. He said quietly, "I would be the last to make fun of you, Donald Fraser, and me knowing the great sorrow in your heart. So what I ask you to do, I ask because there is a reason for it. Just as there is a reason why you should pray in a loud, clear voice."

"But why? The Lord—"

"The Lord," interrupted Wee Alec with a wave of his hand, "will have much on His mind these days, what with the Russians and the Americans and the price of butter going up every day. He never has to trouble Himself much about anything happening in

Cairnsmore. That's why, Donald, you will be certain to speak with a loud, clear voice that He will hear you. And remember, no prayer ever goes unanswered."

Donald frowned. It made sense. And yet—"Aye, but a wee dog, Alec?" he returned doubtfully. "As you said He will be busy what with one thing and another. Do you think He will be minding greatly what happens to a wee dog?"

"He watches over sparrows."

"Sparrows?"

Wee Alec nodded confidently. "It's right in the Bible, lad! It says that not even a sparrow falls but that the good Lord Himself has His eye on it. So if He has His eye on the likes of sparrows it's just good Scots sense that He has His eyes on dogs too." He smiled with his small black eyes. "Especially a Border collie. After all the Lord being the good Shepherd Himself knows more than another the worth of a good sheep dog."

Donald could feel the first stirring of excitement deep within him. Wee Alec was right. But then Wee Alec was always right. How could he have ever doubted it? He gazed at his friend, admiration naked in his eyes.

"Aye, it's the clever one you are for certain, Alec! Och, the clever one indeed."

Wee Alec Logan smiled thinly. "Clever, perhaps, but not wise. Had I been wise I would not have told you this thing. For grief must surely come to Tam when the new dog comes."

But Donald never heard the words. All that mattered was that old Tam would remain. The world which had been black, was suddenly bright again. Bright with a rainbow of shimmering, dancing colors! The world which had been silent as the tomb all at once was bursting with happy sounds. The cry of a whaup as it rose from the marshes by the edge of Loch Lorne. The bright gossip of a hidden brook in the long grass. The distant bark of a dog from over by Ben Appin. A dog. . . .

"Thank you, Alec!" he cried, then he was off and running. "I'll be minding to tell you what happens!"

The little man never moved from where he stood. His troubled eyes followed the rush of the boy across the glen. Only when Donald was lost to sight did Wee Alec Logan stir. Then he turned and grasped the walking cane which leaned against the tree in which he had been perched. The cane was a little too long for him and he held it not by the handle but as one would grip a staff. He made his way slowly back to Cairnsmore.

The troubled look was still in his eyes.

3. A Prayer Is Answered

Nell MacNab looked at the clock in the kitchen and sighed. "Time for your bed, Donald," she said to her son. She picked up the lambskin which she had scraped and cured and which she would later fashion into a pair of slippers for the boy.

From the adjoining room came the quiet steady breathing of his stepfather, already asleep. Finlay MacNab frowned on late hours. A man went to bed early, a man rose early and did his work in the light of God's day.

"Good night, Donald," she said after he had climbed into his wall bed. He felt her lips brush against his hair and the familiar pressure of her hand against his shoulder as she took her leave.

Donald waited for at least ten minutes after his mother had softly closed the door behind her, before drawing back the covers. The only light came from the capering, frolicking flames in the hearth. He could see the outlines of Tam's body as he lay curled up in sleep in his accustomed place by the fire. Small tides of shadow lapped back and forth across the lime-washed walls of the cottage as the flames rose and sank.

Slowly, his heart pounding just a little, Donald slipped out of bed. It had all seemed very fine and wonderful out in Glen Dunan with Wee Alec. It was something else again all by one's self in the room next to where Finlay MacNab was sleeping. Yet it had to be done. And done in a loud, clear voice. That was what Wee Alec had said. And Wee Alec was the cleverest one in all Cairnsmore. Donald closed his eyes. He took a deep, deep breath. . . .

"Oh Lord, I'm minding fine how busy you are what with one thing and another, but Wee Alec says you watch over sparrows and if you watch over sparrows then it's myself is thinking you would not want anything to happen to old Tam here and him a Border collie besides. So maybe you will speak to the heart of Finlay MacNab so that Tam will be spared and—"

Donald got no further. With a crash the door from his stepfather's bedroom flew open. Finlay MacNab took three swift strides into the kitchen. He looked like a fast moving thunderhead about to crash into Ben Appin.

"And what will be the meaning of this, boy?" he thundered. An angry flush suffused his face and neck.

Donald tried to force a matter-of-fact note to his voice. "Oh, and I was only saying my prayers."

"At the top of your lungs?"

The boy retreated. He did not like the angry gleam in Finlay MacNab's eyes. "That was Wee Alec's idea. Wee Alec said the Lord had a lot on His mind these days and I should be sure to speak in a loud, clear voice."

"Wee Alec?" The big shepherd's face darkened. "That sly wee man should mind his own business, I'm thinking! Him and his fancy clothes and fancier talk. So he was the one who told you to go around howling like a banshee in the middle of the night?"

Donald nodded. "Aye, so the Lord would be sure to hear me."

His stepfather's mouth twisted in a sour smile. "Aye, the Lord and Finlay MacNab both."

"Eh?" exclaimed the boy. He was not quite certain he understood. Surely Wee Alec had not told him to pray in a loud, clear voice for Finlay MacNab's benefit? Perhaps it would be best to go on to other things. Things he understood better.

"Wee Alec said that if the Lord kept an eye on the likes of a wee sparrow He would surely notice if one of His Border collies wasn't around, and it a black and white one besides."

A scowl plucked at the loose skin between Finlay MacNab's hard blue eyes. "Well, well. It's plain to see Wee Alec Logan is becoming quite the talker indeed! It's surprised I am he doesn't run for Parliament." The sneer in his voice clung to the words like thick treacle.

"Aye, he's the clever one indeed," Donald said proudly, oblivious of the sarcasm in his stepfather's words. "And Wee Alec says no prayer ever goes without an answer."

Finlay MacNab brought his clenched fist down with a crash on the arm of a chair. "Silence, boy! I've had enough—" He stopped. In the sudden stillness in the room Donald could hear the measured ticking of the big clock on the wall, the sputter and crackle of the burning log in the fireplace. When Finlay MacNab spoke again, all the anger was gone from his voice. He said softly, "Say that again, boy."

Donald ran his tongue over his dry lips. "Wee Alec says no prayer ever goes without an answer."

"Ah," said Finlay MacNab. He stood for a long moment and regarded his stepson. Then he turned and crossed over to the fireplace. He must have seen old Tam sleeping in his place by the fire yet he did not look directly at the dog. Finally he stooped and tossed a handful of bog fir on the red ashes. He watched vacant eyed, as the flames sent a small volley of sparks darting up the blackness of the chimney.

He kept his eyes away from Donald when he spoke.

"A man who loses his faith is a poor man indeed. I would not want you to lose that faith, boy. Aye and because of a dog. Wee Alec, dislike him as I do, was right. The Lord answers prayers. He has answered yours this night."

Donald felt his heart flip over. He tried to separate the words that crowded his throat. "You mean," he cried, "that Tam can stay—?"

"Aye!" All of the old, the familiar harshness burned in Finlay MacNab's voice. "But I do not like this thing that you have done!" He shook his head. "My heart is not such a cold heart, boy, that you must ask the Lord Himself to soften it. The thing that I would have done, I would have done to spare Tam pain. For Tam is a proud dog. Very well then. I will get this other dog. Tam can stay. But no longer will he be *my* dog. No longer will he have a place on the hill. No longer will he have a place by the fire. Good night, Donald."

"Good night," said the boy. His heart was a soaring bird within him, full of wild, joyous songs. Tam would stay after all! His prayer had been answered! Just as Wee Alec had said it would be! Oh Alec, Alec, and how could you have known? But then, are

you not the clever one for certain? In all Cairnsmore none as clever as you! And Tam—Tam would
stay. It was a thought to grasp to one's heart and
croon over!

A thought to fill one's heart so that there was no
room at all for any other thoughts.

Like the thoughts about that other dog that would
be coming to take Tam's place on the hill.

To take Tam's place by the fire.

4. Enter Dandy

It was a week later that Finlay Mac-Nab brought Dandy home.

Dandy was young and handsome. His hair was white and fine spun and his tail swept up in a rich plume behind him. He walked daintily, as befitted his name, as though afraid that at any moment he might step into a puddle and soil his handsome coat. Yet it was plain to see that Dandy, in spite of his genteel mannerisms, was a thoroughbred. He had all the style and the sagacity of the superior working dog. Donald's heart sank when he saw him.

It was strange how in the last several days a hope had taken root within Donald that somehow the new dog would be a disappointment to his stepfather. For if the new dog could not control the sheep then Finlay MacNab would have to go back to old Tam. After all, a good sheep dog would cost no less than twenty-five pounds. It would be impossible for his stepfather to buy another, should the first one prove a failure. In that case Finlay MacNab would just have to go along with old Tam, like it or not. But now, looking gloomily at the cocky newcomer, Donald saw that earlier hope wither like a pale blossom in a cold wind. Dandy was good.

Dandy was more than good. Dandy was class, as Donald found out over the next few weeks while his stepfather trained him. Dandy had the steadfast, beady eye to control, but not frighten the sheep. His movements were sure and confident. He seemed to know the nature of the ewe better than the ewe herself. He never developed the bad habit, common in many dogs, of clopping flat on the ground and crawling along on his stomach towards the alarmed sheep. Perhaps it was simply below Dandy's dignity to soil his beautiful white coat in such a fashion. Perhaps, and Donald sourly agreed, more probably, it was just another instance of Dandy's uncanny knowledge of the nature of sheep.

And Dandy was quick to learn the basic commands also; to lie still; to go out and away from his master; to come back; to go to his left; to go to his right; to go downhill; to go uphill. For each movement Finlay MacNab had a different signal, depending on where he was from his dog. If the wind was blowing strongly against him and the dog could not hear his whistle, the shepherd would signal with a sweep of his arm.

Donald had confidently expected that it would take any newcomer at least three months to learn all of the commands and to execute them properly. But Dandy had amazed him. In the space of what seemed only a few weeks Dandy was making his moves with all of the confidence of a veteran. But then confidence was something the white-haired beauty had never lacked.

On the surface, then, Dandy seemed the perfect sheep dog. Quick, diligent, wise in the way of sheep. Yet perfection in dogs, as in men, is a rare thing. And Dandy, for all his virtues soon revealed one weakness. He was a rabbit chaser.

Had Dandy been any dog other than a sheep dog, it would have mattered very little that he loved to chase rabbits. But for a sheep dog to do so can be a serious and exasperating fault. Should such a dog spot a rabbit on the far side of his sheep, too often he will think nothing of dashing furiously through the sheep after the rabbit. The ewes, scattered and frightened by his wild charge, will take off in all directions. The shepherd then has the difficult and disagreeable task of getting them all together again. Usually the task is not made any easier by the fact that when the dog finally returns, it is tired from its chase over the rough ground.

It was strange, Donald reflected, that the elegant Dandy of all dogs should be a common rabbit chaser. Somehow one would have felt that a dog so regal in his bearing and so proud in his ways would have found it beneath his dignity to even notice a lowly rabbit. Yet there it was. Dandy was a rabbit chaser. Not that he chased them often. Only once in a while. Finlay MacNab had scowled, then conceded that Dandy was a young dog and would learn. Donald was not quite so sure. After all, if Dandy could learn everything else so quickly, why had he been unable to learn not to chase rabbits?

As for old Tam he had continued to go out with Finlay MacNab during Dandy's training. Tam had been a little curious at first about the new dog. In a few days, however, he seemed to forget all about him. He had enough to do taking care of his master's sheep. Every day meant more than eighty miles of running and herding over the rough ground. More than ever he was grateful for the bowl of mash at the end of the day. The bowl of mash and the wicker basket in which he slept in his place by the fire. He had no time for haughty little dogs playing endless games in Glen Dunan.

Then came the day when suddenly it was no longer a game, the day when Finlay MacNab had got up from the breakfast table and tugged his old tweed bonnet down over his head. It was a gesture he made every morning before leaving the cottage. It was the signal for Tam to rise and wait for his master to open the door.

With the familiar tug of the bonnet Tam had slowly gotten to his feet and plodded over to the door. He stood there now, waiting. Waiting as he had waited all his life. Beyond the door was the hill. The hill that his master and he walked every day with the sheep.

For a long moment Finlay MacNab's eyes rested on Tam. Then quietly he said, "Dandy."

At first the old dog had not understood. Only when Finlay MacNab had waved him aside did he move away from the door. Confused, he looked up at his master. But his master was no longer looking at him. It was as though Tam no longer existed.

Dandy, heeding the call, trotted proudly through the door. He held his tail high, like a triumphant banner. Tam's body quivered. Almost as though he was cringing from a blow. His rheumy eyes, wet with the moisture of age, stared blankly at Finlay MacNab as the shepherd followed his new dog outside. There was a metallic click as the door closed behind him.

Donald, silent in his chair by the breakfast table, watched the little drama with suddenly troubled eyes. He had expected that Tam would be disappointed when he no longer would go out to look the hill with his master. Only he had not expected the old dog would take it quite so badly. Tam was slumped forward by the closed door. His wrinkled muzzle was lost somewhere between his two front paws. His eyes were fixed on the door. He made no sound.

The boy crossed over and dropped to his knees beside Tam. He pressed his face against the coarseness of the dog's coat. He could feel the slow rise and fall of Tam's body against his cheek.

"Oh, and it will be all right, Tam, and just you see if it won't," he said in a half croon, half whisper. "Besides there's no sense at all, at all in fretting because Finlay MacNab will look the hill with a new dog. Wee Alec says that's the way the world is, Tam. And there's none as clever as Wee Alec in all Cairnsmore."

It was only when he had spoken his name that Donald remembered. What was it he had said? *The proud suffer more.* Wee Alec had known what would happen when Tam would no longer go out with Finlay MacNab.

The proud suffer more. Almost Donald could read the quiet pain in Tam's eyes. For the first time the boy felt the first stirrings of doubt deep within his heart.

Perhaps it would have been better after all to have done nothing. To have let Finlay MacNab do with his dog as he had wanted to do in the first place.

5. The Way the World Is

Two days later Finlay MacNab moved Tam from his place by the fire.

"My dog must know he is my dog," Donald's stepfather had said shortly when he had caught the boy's eyes regarding him. "When you are older, boy, you will understand such things. Why I must have one dog just. Dandy is now my dog. He walks alone by my side in the day. He rests alone by my side at night."

"Aye," muttered Donald. He remembered Wee Alec having said something like that. Something

about Finlay MacNab being one of those shepherds
who shared his comforts with his dog as he shared
his work. It had been hard to understand then. It
was even harder now.

"It's yourself will be minding fine," Donald
pointed out, "that this has always been Tam's place.
Right here by the fire."

"I'm minding that."

"I'm thinking Tam will take it sore if you move
him."

Finlay MacNab's eyes were granite hard. "I would
have spared him this, boy. Do not forget that. But
there will be no other way. Not if Dandy is to know
that he is really my dog. As he *must* know." He
paused, then added, "As once Tam was my dog."

Donald started to answer but bit back the words
deep in his throat. What use was there to plead with
this man? This man so cold. So remote. So sure of
his own righteousness.

He waited until Finlay MacNab had gone out
before appealing to his mother. Surely she would
understand. But Nell MacNab had only shaken her
head.

"You must know, lad, that your father works hard
for our bread." She pushed aside the oatmeal she
was using to make the bannocks for their supper.

"He needs a dog to earn that bread. He has chosen that dog. Dandy."

"Aye, but Tam—"

She sighed. "That is the way the world is, Donald."

He started. *That is the way the world is.* The same words again. Somehow the more he learned of this world the more it saddened him. Quite plainly it wasn't a world for dogs. At least old dogs who were no longer needed.

"Oh and I'm sorry, Donald." It was his mother again. She must have read the bitterness and the misery in his eyes. He felt the quick pressure of her fingers on his arm. Suddenly the familiar warm scent

of her hair was a closeness against his face. "Laddie, laddie," she whispered. "Well I know that you love Tam. And so do I. Aye, and so does your father if you could only know. That was why he wanted to spare him the pain he knew would come when another dog would take Tam's place. And I'm fearing this is only the beginning." She moved her lips across his hair. "Perhaps it would have been kinder, Donald, if you had not—" She stopped and left the rest of the thought unspoken.

There are some thoughts best left unspoken.

With Dandy taking over Tam's place by the fire, alongside Finlay MacNab's chair, the old dog retreated to a spot at the back of the kitchen, next to the dresser. From there in the evening after Finlay MacNab and Dandy had come home, he would lie and stare blankly at the fire. At the yellow sparks leap-frogging up the chimney. At the place where Dandy lay curled up by the fire at the slippered feet of Finlay MacNab.

Seldom did Tam leave the cottage now that he was no longer needed. And no matter how Donald might coax him, he scarcely touched the food that the boy set before him. It was as though he had lost all interest in living. How he could survive at all

on the few mouthfuls of gruel he swallowed every
two or three days, the boy could only guess. Finally,
with the passing of the weeks and the long winter
months, Tam seemed no more than a small heap of
bones and straggly hair as he lay in his wicker basket
next to the dresser. No more than that. Unless one
counted the two big eyes that lay deep in the skull
like two hot coals.

The eyes that stared unwinkingly at the fireplace
where Dandy lay at the feet of Finlay MacNab.

6. *Left on the Hill*

It was a clear crisp morning in early April when Donald ran into Wee Alec Logan coming out of the High Street office of the Cairnsmore *Weekly Press*. Wee Alec not only wrote the stories but he delivered the papers as well. There was a stack of them under his arm now. He seemed grateful for the opportunity to place them on the ground and to smooth the wrinkles from the sleeve of his sports jacket.

"Ah, Donald! You're quite the stranger! Haven't seen you at all since before the winter. A bad one, wasn't it? Well it's gone now and good riddance to it." He perched on tiptoe and drank in a lungful of the spring-soft air. "I was beginning to think the sun had forgotten all about us here in Scotland. For the last five months all we've had has been snow and fog, plus a little rain to break the monotony." He smiled with his small black eyes.

Donald nodded listlessly. "That will be right, Alec. It was a bad one for certain."

The little man looked at him quickly. "There are some who say that in Scotland we get eight months of winter and four months of wind and rain. The rest is summer." He chuckled. "Not a word about spring, mind you! Well, it's not quite that bad. It's just that the first of April usually arrives in Scotland around the first of June."

"Aye," said Donald. He was thinking that spring, no matter when it came, would hardly be the same without Tam walking the hill with Finlay MacNab.

Alec's shrewd eyes studied the boy. "And how is Tam?" he asked quietly.

Donald shook his head. He did not answer.

"I see. H-mm. You will remember, lad. I was afraid of this. And Dandy?"

"The same one is fine." Donald returned shortly.

"He is clever then with the sheep?"

The boy moved a shoulder. "Aye, he is that. Finlay MacNab claims he has never seen his likes for the quick learning." He could not deny the edge of bitterness that tinged his words.

Wee Alec said, "He has a good conceit of himself, has Dandy. I have seen him with the sheep. Still he is a clever one." He paused. "It would seem then that he no longer runs around with his rabbit friends?"

Again Donald shrugged. "Finlay MacNab hasn't said anything about it lately. I'm thinking he will not be chasing them anymore. Anyway it's not Dandy I'm worried about. It's Tam. He's just a heap of skin and bones."

The little man frowned and looked away. He was silent for a long moment. "I am sorry about that, Donald. Finlay MacNab knew his dog after all. That is why he would have spared him this."

"Aye," said Donald, "it's the kind man he is for certain." He could feel the sourness in his mouth as his tongue brushed the words.

The little man shook his head. "I am afraid, lad, you are not quite fair to him. His life has not been an easy one. He does only what he thinks is best. When problems come along in this life you will learn, Donald, that the easy way out of them is not always the right way. Finlay MacNab is not the man to choose the easy way. When you grow up to be a man, lad, like Wee Alec Logan himself—" a wry smile bent his lips—"you will be minding that. Well, I'll say good-by for now, Donald. Got work to do. Lately it's been taking us a month to get the *Weekly Press* out. Even for Cairnsmore that will be some kind of record."

"Good-by, Alec," said the boy. He waved after the retreating figure of the dapper little man. He knew Wee Alec meant well. Still it was plain to see that even Alec, clever as he was, could be wrong about some things. Like Finlay MacNab for instance. Aye, and it was daft for certain to think that his stepfather had been worried at all about easy ways and hard ways when it had come to old Tam. Right from the beginning there had only been one way. Just as there was only one way in everything he did. The way that suited Finlay MacNab best. The scowl on Donald's face darkened. It was still there, darker than ever, when he got to the peat hags to replenish their fuel supply.

The peats had already been "stripped" by Finlay MacNab. The absence of the thick, matted top layer of heather roots and turf made it easier for the boy to work. He cut and tossed aside the spongy choco-

late brown slices with the easy rhythm of the prac-
ticed cutter. As the peats hit the ground the released
scent of crushed bog myrtle filled his nostrils.

Normally Donald enjoyed cutting peats. The
knowledge that each peat would bring warmth to
their cottage somehow brought a similar warmth
to his heart. But today it was different. There was
little warmth to be got from the realization that old
Tam would never again have his place by the fire.

Donald had been working steadily for almost three
hours when he suddenly became aware of the cold-
ness in the air. He sleeved the sweat from his face
and stood quite still. The wind from the north had

a keen, thin bite to it. The kind of bite that comes just before onrushing snows in January. Yet this was April and not January. And it had only been a few hours ago that the sky had been clear and bright.

Donald felt a shiver snake down his back. Perhaps from the sudden cold. Perhaps from something else. The thought of the dangers that lurked in these unpredictable early April storms. For April was the lambing time. Many of the ewes, weary at best from the rigors of the long winter, would have a difficult time if the lambs came at the same time as a spring snow. Aye, thought Donald grimly, and so would their lambs. The boy looked up uneasily at the sky.

Dark shreds of cloud scudded southwards, loping like lean gray wolves before some unseen demon over the horizon. A cluster of spindly rowan trees shivered in the wind and beat their boughs together as though for warmth. Away in the distance Donald could see Loch Lorne. Under the tormenting wind the lake snarled and curled a long white lip. The whole scene, as far as the eye could see, was one of gloom and impending storm.

Hesitating no longer, Donald set out for home with his sack of freshly cut peats. The wind was now icy cold and the sky one long low expanse of grayness. He had almost gained the safety of the cottage when the snow came, small sharp pellets that stung his face like a host of tiny needles.

"Donald!" His mother looked up quickly from her mending. Her face was anxious. "I'm glad you're home, lad."

"Aye, no less than me," he said as he warmed his hands by the fire. He grinned in an effort to dispel the worried look on his mother's face. "Wee Alec was saying something just this morning about April never getting to Scotland before June. I'm thinking he meant July."

She nodded but he had the feeling she had not heard him. The tension was still in her eyes, and her mouth. She said, "Your father went out to bring the sheep down when he got the word on the wireless that the storm was coming. He's out there now."

"Aye," he said. He was a little surprised she had bothered to mention it. Finlay MacNab's place was with his sheep. All of the other shepherds around Cairnsmore would be out looking after theirs too.

She rose slowly and, laying down her needle, crossed over to the window where she stood staring out at the snow. "It could be a bad one," she said. "These late storms are always the bad ones." Her eyes stared out at the swirling snow beyond the window. Her lips moved soundlessly. Perhaps in prayer.

The boy suddenly looked around. He had forgotten all about Tam. The old dog lay curled up at the foot of the dresser. He stared vacantly at the fire. He seemed scarcely to have stirred for the past week. Seeing Tam reminded Donald of someone else. He looked over at the empty box by the fire. But of course he should have known. Dandy would be out with Finlay MacNab. If ever a shepherd needed his dog it was on a day like this.

"Dandy—" he began for something to say. He glanced over at his mother. He did not like the cleft of worry that persisted between her gray eyes.

"Where else?" She returned. She passed him a

mug of hot tea. It was dark, the way Donald always liked it, with plenty of sugar and a top taste of peat smoke from the fire. He sipped it slowly, grateful for its warmth. Outside the wind seemed to increase in fury. The snow dropping down from the low sky was one long silent wall of whiteness, a wall without end and without beginning.

Nell MacNab moved her spoon absently around her cup. She said, "And about that, Donald. Well I know how you felt about Dandy coming here. But it's yourself must admit the same one has been a good dog. Aye, a grand dog for certain and with a smart way to him."

"Aye." Donald answered reluctantly. There was no denying his mother's words were true. Finlay MacNab was not a man who gave praise easily. And Finlay MacNab had praised Dandy. Not in so many words, of course. That was not his way. He had simply said, "Dandy will do." He did not have to say more. It was plain to see he was pleased with the dog. Dandy had come through the winter with flying colors. The sheep respected and obeyed the young dog. "Dandy will do," Finlay MacNab had said. No, he did not have to say more.

As the hours passed, the freakish storm grew in

fury. The wind now was one long banshee wail that set the window panes to endless trembling. Suddenly Donald caught his mother's eye flitting to the wag-o'-the-wall clock, ticking quietly above the fireplace. It was only then that Donald realized Finlay MacNab was late.

Something was wrong. Finlay MacNab was never late. His stepfather was a man of fixed habits and set ways. So many minutes to do this task. So many minutes to do that. Time was a gift that God had given man in His goodness. Finlay MacNab shepherded the Lord's minutes with the same care that he shepherded Colonel Chisholm's sheep.

Yes, Finlay MacNab was late. And Finlay MacNab was never late. Even during the two big snowstorms that had struck Cairnsmore during the past winter, he had always done what he had to do and come home on time. After all, it had only been a matter of keeping the sheep together and getting them down from the hills to the safety of the four-foot dry, stone dike and where the lie of the land afforded shelter from the fierce winds. Only Finlay MacNab was late today. Something was wrong.

Donald tugged on his boots. "I'll see what will be keeping him," he said shortly. He knew his stepfather as a man who would never ask for help from another. Yet something was plainly amiss. Besides it was difficult to sit here doing nothing.

"You will not be going out after him, lad?" his mother cried. "There's no need, at all, at all. Besides Dandy is with him. Dandy has been just grand with the sheep all winter, your father said so himself. You will be minding how he said 'Dandy will do.' Your father would not have said that if it wasn't so."

"Still he's not here," Donald said stubbornly. He shrugged on his heavy coat and looked over at Tam. The old dog lay in his wicker basket next to the dresser. His face was lost in the shadows but Donald knew the dog was there. Tam seldom moved from that spot any more. If it was not for the light that still glowed in his deep-set eyes one might have thought him dead.

The boy hesitated. He would have liked to take Tam with him. Only his stepfather might not understand at all. He had seen Finlay MacNab when he was angry. No, better leave the old dog where he was. Besides Dandy was out there with him now. Dandy—

Crash!

Donald jumped as the door was flung back against the stopper. There was a quick rush of cold air. The boy spun around. Finlay MacNab stood framed in the doorway. His head was bowed as though with exhaustion. His shoulders were stooped, heavy with snow. He stood for a long moment, motionless. Then his right hand moved and the door slammed shut behind him. It was only then that Donald realized Dandy was not with him.

The boy stared. "Dandy!" he cried. "Where's Dandy?"

The shepherd drew his hand across his eyes, scarred with weariness. His lips moved just wide enough to let the word through. "Gone."

"Gone?" gasped Donald and his mother together.

Finlay MacNab slumped forward on a chair, his head cradled between his hands. After several moments he looked up. His bleak eyes were a barometer of his fatigue. "Gone," he repeated bitterly. His mouth jerked in a spasm of pain. "He saw a rabbit in the snow. He—" Finlay MacNab did not finish the sentence. He did not have to finish it. Donald's eyes found his mother's. So he had been right after all. Dandy had finally fallen victim to his one weakness. Rabbit chasing.

Donald knew he should have felt a glow of satisfaction. Yet there was none. Dislike his stepfather as he might he still could not help but feel a stab of pity for the crushed figure slumped forward on the chair.

"And the sheep?" It was Nell MacNab who asked the question.

"Scattered. Dandy went right through them after the rabbit." He shook his head. "He left me on the hill."

He left me on the hill. Donald felt his heart skip a beat. Dandy had committed the one cardinal sin of a sheep dog. He had left his master to tend the sheep for himself. And in a storm like this—

"I got most of them down. But there's a number of them still up there. I'm not knowing where. If only Dandy—" The old shepherd shook his head.

Donald never knew where the words came from but they were there on his lips and he spoke them.

"There's Tam," he ventured.

Finlay MacNab's long head went up. "Eh?"

"There's Tam," the boy said again.

"Tam?" The shepherd's eyes strayed to the place by the fire that had once been Tam's place. Then he seemed to remember. His glance probed the darkness by the floor at the foot of the dresser. "Tam?" he muttered.

It had only been a question. Nothing more than that. The voice that had carried it had been old and

made small and tight with weariness. Yet not too old
that two ears did not lift in the shadows. Not too
small that two eyes did not suddenly brighten. Not
too tight with weariness that a tail did not lift and
beat a weak tattoo on the floor. With a soft little
whinny Tam got to his feet. Head low, ears back,
he made his way across the kitchen to where his
master sat. From where his master had called his
name. The old dog rested his chin against Finlay's
boots and waited. Just as he had waited in the old
days when there had been only the two of them and
they had walked the hill together.

Finlay MacNab's face was a battlefield of con-
flicting emotions. Surprise was there and resentment.
Pity was there, and distrust. Watching his stepfather's face Donald could only guess at the struggle
within him. To take Tam out with him now was to
admit he had been wrong. And Finlay MacNab was
never wrong.

No one moved. Donald stood by the door. Nell
MacNab had crossed over to her husband. Her eyes
were bright, perhaps from tears, perhaps from the
smoke from the fireplace. Her fingers pressed Finlay's shoulders, wet with melting snow. Tam lay
where he was at the foot of the one he loved best.
Had never ceased to love.

It was Nell MacNab who spoke first. "The sheep, Finlay," she said quietly. "They will be needing you —and Tam."

Donald darted a quick glance of wonder at his mother. Of all the words in all of the world, by what wisdom had she known that the words just spoken had been the right words, the only words? Perhaps it was simply that mothers have a special wisdom all their own. Perhaps that was it.

The knuckles showed white on Finlay MacNab's clenched hands. Then slowly the hard pride died in the fierce blue eyes. The hands unclenched. For above all else Finlay was the good shepherd. And the good shepherd is faithful to his sheep.

He tugged his old bonnet down over his head, in the familiar gesture. "Come, Tam," he said, as he had said a thousand times in the old days. "I'm thinking we'd better be off to look the hill, you and me."

Tam was on his feet the moment he reached for the bonnet. He wrinkled his nose and showed his small dagger teeth. Almost as though he was grinning about something. His bushy tail swayed like the sporran of a Highlander's kilt as he trotted jauntily over to the door.

"If you're not minding at all," said Donald hesitantly, "maybe I can help a wee bit with the sheep."

The loose skin over Finlay MacNab's eyes bunched together in a scowl. He opened his mouth angrily then seemed to ease back on the trigger of his quick temper. He studied his stepson as though seeing him for the first time. His stern lips bent at the corners. Almost as though he were smiling. But then *that* was impossible. Finlay MacNab *never* smiled.

He turned his back on the boy. "Come along, Tam," he ordered in his gruff voice. Then when the dog had trotted out, "You too, Donald."

He looked back over his shoulder at Nell MacNab before following the boy outside.

His lips were still loose at the corners in the ghost of a smile as he drew the door behind him.

7. The Storm

Donald struggled behind his step-father and Tam. The air was full of flying snow so that it was difficult for him to face the wind and draw breath. He kept his head low and sheathed his eyes against the stinging icy pellets. When they finally got to the lower reaches of Ben Appin, Finlay MacNab halted. Above them the mountain commenced its sharp rise into a white nothingness. It seemed to tower directly overhead, for all the world like a huge iceberg that had suddenly swirled silently out of the mist and snow and would crash down on them at any moment.

"Donald!" Finlay MacNab was speaking. The wind tore at his words and it was hard for Donald to hear them. "You—Tam—the wee burn at the foot of the glen—ice—" He gasped for breath then swung his arm wide in the characteristic sweep of the shepherd. "I'll go wide—meet you—" He turned his back on the wind and cried something to Tam that Donald did not catch. The next moment he was gone, lost in the swirling snow.

Donald hesitated for a moment and peered through the snowflakes at the little collie. Would old Tam be up to such a trip? After all, he was no longer the Tam who had gone out each morning to look the hill with Finlay MacNab. The long stay indoors had taken its toll. So had his failure to eat more than a few scraps of food. Regarding him now, Donald could see how his ribs protruded to form an arch, for all the world like the newly laid keel of a boat. Only the eyes had not changed. The eyes that snapped with excitement as they looked up at the boy. He hesitated no longer.

"This way, Tam!" he cried. He plunged ahead avoiding the drifts, his eyes straining through the falling snow for any of the lost sheep. Together they fought their way around the flank of Ben Appin, stumbling and slipping over the treacherous surface.

The burn of which Finlay MacNab had spoken was several miles somewhere to their right. Very possibly the little stream was already frozen. If so the sheep, afraid of ice, might well be huddled by the bank. On the other hand, the lack of protection from the storm on this side of the burn, might have forced them, against their wills, across the stream. If the ice was firm enough they would have gotten across without difficulty. If not—Donald groaned seeing the scene in his mind's eye. The ice, which might be strong enough to support one or two sheep crossing separately, might not be strong enough if they bunched and charged across in a panic. If that happened and the sheep fell through the ice, disaster would almost surely follow. The sheep, heavy with their winter wool, would soak up the water and drown. Even if some were able to struggle across, it was doubtful that with their water-soaked wool, they would have the strength to scramble up the small slope on the far side. Donald shook his head angrily to dismiss the unpleasant thoughts that clung like so many burrs to his mind. Better not to think such thoughts. He slitted his eyes against the sleet and followed his feet across the snow.

He had been fighting his way around Ben Appin for almost two hours when suddenly, with the same swiftness with which it had come, the storm blew itself out across Glen Dunan. In the quick stillness after the shrieking of the wind, Donald could almost hear his heart beat. Here and there little clusters of snowflakes churned in the still air, like so many aimless butterflies. Donald stared up at the sky. It was lifting. Far to the west a sharp sliver of brightness cut across the mass of gray clouds. The storm was over.

Donald looked around him. Like a battlefield after the fighting had ceased, signs of the fierce struggle lay at every side. As far as the eye could see was an endless sweep of whiteness. Here and there wounded branches drooped earthwards, each with its bandage of snow around it. A few trees were bent all the way over, their crowns sweeping the ground. The only odd note was lent by a handful of dwarf spruce trees nearby. In their thick headdresses of snow they looked like nothing so much as a party of wizened old ladies in bright wigs setting out for tea.

Grateful that the storm had lifted, Donald set about the task of finding the sheep, with renewed hope. At least he could see where he was going now.

When they finally reached the frozen stream at the bottom of the glen, Donald felt his heart sink. There was not a sheep in sight! He had been certain that some of them would have taken refuge there. Unless they had tried to cross the ice. . . .

He jerked his head up and stared at the burn, a cold sweat in the palms of his hands. If they had tried to cross and the ice had broken— But the ice had not broken! He let the pent-up air out softly in a long, slow sigh of relief. Wherever the sheep were, they were not in the stream. But where were they?

It was Tam, alert and bright-eyed who noticed the steam rising from the holes in the snow. Taut as a pointer, his head high, his right foreleg raised slightly, the old dog gazed fixedly at the tiny ribbon of steam rising from the ground. Finally, a small growl broke from his throat and rushing forward he buried his muzzle deep in the snow.

"Tam! Have you gone daft?" cried Donald as the little collie started to thresh at the snow with flying feet. Then all of a sudden the boy caught a flash of movement on the surface of the snow. Almost as though there was something underneath. . . .

"Tam! You've found one!" he exclaimed. He threw himself beside the dog and flailed wildly with his hands. He felt them brush against something coarse and solid. Something that stirred under his touch. The next moment the sheep was free and cradled in his arms.

Together they dug out six more ewes from the snow nearby. Each one that they found was lying in a hollow place about twice its size. Donald reasoned that the heat from the ewe's body had melted the snow around her. The steam that Tam had no-

ticed had come from the sheep's warm breath rising and striking the cold upper air. No doubt the sheep had huddled together in front of the stream. Those on the outside had feared to cross the ice. The sheep on the inside had stayed where they were and had been gradually covered by the drifting snow. Another half hour and they would surely have died. If it had not been for Tam. . . .

The boy turned and stared hard at the dog. How had old Tam known? But then Tam was wise. The wisest sheep dog in all the countryside around Cairnsmore.

The boy followed the dog after that. It was plain as the nose on his face that Tam knew a lot more about sheep than he did. And it was equally plain that Tam knew what the problem was. "Find them," was all Donald urged, and Tam was off, his head low, his ears flat. Where the old dog got his strength from Donald could only guess. Perhaps it was not strength really. Perhaps it was something else. Spirit. Spirit, that fierce white flame deep inside a man— or a dog—that drives him beyond the frontiers of his normal endurance.

It was Tam who found a score of the sheep down by the boggy sedges of Loch Lorne. They had apparently sought a sheltered spot away from the cruel wind. They had escaped the wind all right only to find themselves mired down in the slush. Heavy with their lambs and their wool the ewes had gradually given up the struggle. They lay, some on their backs, and waited for death to come. A number of those on their backs were already dead when Donald and Tam reached them, their bodies cold and stiff. The boy worked frantically to free the others. He clawed at the slush and mud like one possessed. Sixteen of them were still alive when he dragged them out of the marshland to firm ground.

They found more—or rather Tam did—up on the lee of Ben Appin, huddled together by a large cairn of stones. Some, with a wisdom rare in sheep, had taken up lodging in the ruins of an old castle. Despite himself, Donald had grinned when he saw them. Seldom do sheep look regal. Only *these* looked regal. Protected from the storm as they had been, they were quite dry. The leader, a haughty old girl, seemed to be acting the part of some ancient Highland chief's lady as she greeted them at the door with a soft *baa* of welcome. Tam, who had a no-nonsense attitude in these matters, put an end to the playacting by briskly routing them out of their sanctuary. When Finlay MacNab finally got together with Donald near the burn he stared in unbelief at the flock strung out before the boy and the dog.

"It's not to be believed at all!" he muttered. His eyes traveled from the half dozen sheep he was driving to the three score that Donald was bringing in. "And where did you find them, boy?" he demanded gruffly. Not for worlds would Finlay Mac-Nab have shown pleasure. Yet if pleasure was not in his voice and expression it was in his eyes. A pleasure and relief impossible to hide. For these were his sheep. And the good shepherd loves his sheep.

"Eh?" inquired Donald innocently. "Oh, and it wasn't me at all that found them. It was Tam."

Finlay MacNab frowned. "Tam?"

"The same one. And after all, and why not? Has he not looked the hill with you all his life? There will be no other dog knows the sheep and their daft ways like Tam." Donald did not try to keep the note of pride from his voice.

The frown on his stepfather's face darkened to a scowl. Too late Donald realized that in praising Tam he had criticized Finlay MacNab. And Finlay Mac-Nab was not one to take lightly to criticism. Particularly from a boy. His pale blue eyes flashed. Then with an effort he seemed to check himself. He said quietly, as though he had not heard what Donald had just said, "Away and take the sheep down, boy. They should be no trouble at all."

Donald nodded, hesitated. "And Tam?"

"Tam?" Finlay MacNab turned his head aside so that he did not have to face his stepson. "What else, boy?" he snapped. "There are other sheep to be found." He tugged at his old bonnet and took a firmer grip on his shepherd's crook. "Come away, Tam. We'll take another look at the hill, you and me."

It was hard to know why all of a sudden his eyes should be wet. Snowflakes, of course. Angrily Donald drew his sleeve across his face and stared after them. They climbed the small brae together. Just as they had climbed many a small brae together in the old days. Finlay in front, Tam trotting contentedly at his heels, his ears and tail high.

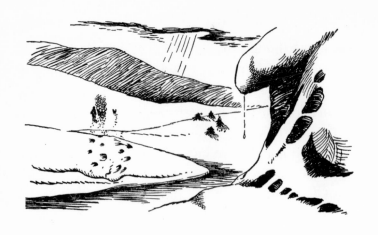

8. A Place by the Fire

It was not until the evening of the following day that Dandy came home. He practically slunk into the kitchen on his stomach, his ears flat and his tail dragging on the floor. Donald stared. It was hard to believe that this was the same Dandy he knew. Gone was all the cockiness and swagger. Poor Dandy! Donald had never seen such a woebegone excuse for a sheep dog. Dandy crawled over to where Finlay MacNab sat in his big chair and rested his chin on his master's slippered feet.

Donald laid down the split bamboo salmon rod

on which he was working and waited for the fire-
works to start. He knew at first hand something of
Finlay MacNab's capacity for anger, even when the
provocation was slight. But what Dandy had done
had been far from slight. He had committed the one
unpardonable crime. He had deserted his master.

More than that he had scattered the sheep. A quick
pity flooded the boy's heart for the young dog as
Finlay MacNab laid aside his glasses and rose slowly
to his feet.

Donald waited for the lightning to strike. But it
did not strike. For fully thirty seconds the gaunt,
round-shouldered old shepherd gazed down at
Dandy, contrite at his feet. When Finlay MacNab
finally spoke there was no anger in his voice, no

scorn. Only a note of gentle wonder. "Well, well, and so it's yourself, Dandy, come home to old Finlay," he said. "You that was as proud as a piper and a fine conceit to you, and now look at you." He shook his head sadly. "But fine I'm minding, Dandy, that we all will have our faults, beasts and men alike. Yours is chasing after the rabbits. Mine—" He left the rest of the sentence unspoken. He closed his eyes.

"Away with you, Finlay MacNab!" snapped Donald's mother. "There will be no need at all—" She stopped as the metallic thud of the knocker sounded through the kitchen. She frowned and looked at the clock. "And who will be paying us a visit at this time of night?" She opened the door. "Well, and it's yourself, Colonel Chisholm," she exclaimed. "But come in! Come in! You're just in time for tea."

"Thank you, Nell," returned the visitor. "Hope you don't mind my popping in like this. A few things I wanted to talk over with Finlay here."

The boy retreated a few steps while his stepfather waved his employer to a chair. Donald liked Colonel Chisholm. His fierce red moustache, a legacy of his service in the Black Watch during the war, swept upwards at the ends for all the world like a set of horns. It was the only thing really menacing about the colonel. His long face was a landscape of prominent bones dominated by a great beak of a nose. Because of the big moustache which concealed his mouth it was hard to know when the colonel was smiling. That is, if one did not notice the colonel's eyes. They lay like two round blue pools deep below a great overhang of shaggy brow. When the colonel smiled lights flashed in the round blue pools. They were there often. They were there now.

"Thank you, Nell," he said as he accepted the cup from Donald's mother. He took a long slow sip of the beverage. "Ah! I have always said that there is no one in Cairnsmore can make a better cup of tea than you, Nell MacNab."

Donald's mother colored with pleasure. "Away with you, Colonel!" she exclaimed in a small fluster.

"Tell me, Nell," he pressed, with a wink in Donald's direction, "I promise not to reveal your secret to a soul. What *do* you put in it to make it taste so good?"

"Tea," Nell replied bluntly.

"Tea?" The small lights winked deep in the colonel's eyes. "So that's your secret?" He took a few more sips. "Nothing like a good cup of tea."

"Unless it's another," Donald's mother said. She lifted the tea cosy from the pot and filled the colonel's cup. From one of her secret hiding places, to which she resorted when special visitors came, she brought out a tin of biscuits. Donald was always amazed at the number of such hiding places in the small cottage. There were never any biscuits around when *he* looked. Yet his mother never failed to come up with all sorts of delicacies when callers such as Colonel Chisholm dropped in.

Finlay MacNab frowned. Quite obviously he did not care for all this small talk. He cleared his throat. "I've been thinking, Colonel Chisholm," he said drily, "you will not have come here this night to learn how to make a cup of tea."

"That's right, Finlay." The colonel placed his cup on the table and leaned back in his chair. He was all business now. "Quite a storm we had."

The old shepherd moved his head slightly. "Aye."

"I understand we lost a number of sheep." The colonel's searching eyes did not leave his shepherd's face.

Donald looked up quickly. So that was why the colonel was here! He had heard then about the sheep that had been lost down by Loch Lorne. The boy traded an anxious glance with his mother. He hoped that there would be no trouble because of the dead sheep. For while he knew Colonel Chisholm could be the most pleasant of men, he was no fool. He ran an efficient business and followed a strictly no-nonsense approach where his company profits were concerned.

Finlay MacNab said guardedly, "Aye, we lost some."

"How many?"

The old shepherd looked down at his big hands. Then his shoulders lifted and he stared almost defiantly at his employer. "Ten."

"Ten?" Colonel Chisholm's eyebrows went up.

He darted a suspicious glance at the other. "Are you sure of that?"

Finlay's lips tightened. "I will not be a man who treats truth lightly, Colonel Chisholm," he said, an indignant glint in his eyes.

"That is true." The colonel tugged at one end of his fierce red moustache. "So you lost ten, eh?"

Finlay nodded unhappily. "Fine you know I am sorry about it." He swallowed. "You placed me in charge of them. And I lost ten."

The colonel grinned. "Congratulations."

"Eh?"

"I said congratulations!"

"Congratulations?" Finlay's brow darkened and the old fire returned to his blue eyes. "Is this some kind of joke?"

"No joke, Finlay. You see, if we only lost ten we did a lot better than any of the others around here. Jock Drummond lost forty. The Argyle farm has fifty dead and missing. Andrew Simpson, with the smallest flock of them all, still managed to lose thirty. So that's why I said congratulations! You turned in the best job of any of the shepherds around Cairnsmore. Needless to say, Finlay, I'm most grateful."

Finlay MacNab took a deep breath and gazed down at his clenched hands. "It's only fair I should

tell you just the same. I should not have lost the ten."

"Away with you, man!" snapped the colonel. He suddenly laughed and smacked his thigh with a big red hand. "And that idiot Jenkins, my factor! You'll not believe this, Finlay, but it was only last week he was after me to give you something easier to do. You know, like keeping the records of the sales. Said you were getting too old to be going out with the sheep." The colonel snorted. "Idiot!" he exclaimed again.

Donald's eyes were fixed on his stepfather. Finlay MacNab's face was expressionless. Only the big hands suddenly tense against the arms of his chair betrayed him. He said slowly, "Too old? Me?" He looked at his visitor. There was fear in his eyes.

The colonel nodded vigorously. "I told you the man was an idiot!" He extended his tea cup. "Thanks, Nell, I will have another." His brows mashed in a frown. " 'Need to get a younger man, Colonel.' That's what Jenkins said. As though good shepherds were picked up on grocery shelves like cans of corned beef!"

Finlay MacNab did not appear to have heard him. He said, as though to himself, "Too old?"

"An idiot!" The colonel barked again. "If he wasn't

the best factor around I'd give him the sack! Besides what would a man like you do behind a desk, eh? Tell me that now! Why, you'd go out of your mind, man, you that have spent your whole life on the hills with the sheep." Again he brought a big ham-like hand down hard on his thigh. "And that's what I told that idiot Jenkins! Of course that was before *this*. Can't wait till I tell him we lost fewer sheep than anyone around Cairnsmore!"

Finlay MacNab did not answer. He stared into the flames, a faraway look in his eyes. When he spoke he spoke softly, without any of the usual fire in his voice. "So the factor is after thinking I'm too old to look the hill any more? Well, well, and perhaps the man is right. Fine I know I'm not as young as I was—"

"Who is?" interrupted Colonel Chisholm loudly. He tugged again at his fierce moustache. "Do you think that idiot Jenkins is getting any younger, eh? Do you think I'm getting any younger? Of course not! Furthermore, I'm going to tell you something, Finlay MacNab. It's not a question of age. It's how well a man knows his job! And the spirit with which he does that job!"

Finlay MacNab nodded. "Spirit," he repeated, to no one in particular. He hesitated, then slanted a glance in Donald's direction. "By the way, Colonel, would you be interested at all in having a dog? You'll be minding I've had two of them for a while now. I thought to give one away but I knew that nobody at all in the village would have him, him being so old besides. I was thinking that a man like yourself now could use an extra dog."

Donald felt the slow wash of sickness deep in his stomach. So that was it! His stepfather had finally found someone to take Tam! No wonder Finlay Mac-Nab had been so gentle and forgiving when Dandy had crawled home! It wasn't in Finlay MacNab's nature to be gentle and forgiving. There had to be a reason. Now the reason was plain to see. Despite Dandy's desertion, despite Tam's noble work in saving the sheep, Finlay MacNab was still Finlay MacNab. Proud and stubborn and thick-headed. The bitterness in Donald's heart rose in a quick tide to his eyes as he stared at this man who was his stepfather.

Colonel Chisholm frowned as he got to his feet. "Tam? He was a grand dog, of course. He was—"

"He *is* a grand dog," Finlay MacNab cut in. "And he'll be a grand dog to the day he dies."

"Hm. I see. So why do you want me to take him?"

"It's not Tam I'm giving away now, Colonel," Finlay said quietly. "It's Dandy."

"Dandy? The new dog? But you only got him a little while ago. I had heard he was a smart little fellow."

"He is," responded the shepherd quickly. "Aye. Smart as you say, Colonel. None smarter. Only— only he's not Tam." He paused. "What was it you said a wee while ago? It's how well a man knows his job. And the spirit with which he does it." His thin lips flattened in what might have been a smile. "Perhaps, Colonel Chisholm, that will be no less true of dogs than it will be of men."

The colonel laughed. "You know best. I've got too much good Scots blood in me to pass up a bargain when I see it." He scooped up Dandy in his big hands and trailed his finger between his ears. "Come along, Dandy. Time you and I were getting home." He turned at the door. "Good night, Nell, Donald. And—and thanks, Finlay. Ten sheep you say? Can't get over it. That idiot Jenkins—" The crash of the door swallowed up the rest of the words.

Finlay MacNab sat motionless, his hands clasped. In the flickering light from the lamp Donald noticed for the first time how deep were the lines around his eyes and mouth. How streaked with silver his hair. How bowed his shoulders.

Nell MacNab did not speak. Neither did Donald. They watched him as he gripped the arms of his chair and slowly got to his feet. He walked stiffly over to the dresser and when he got there he stooped down. Then he picked up the little wicker basket with Tam in it and laid it down gently in a place that Donald knew.

A place by the fire.